MAN
IN THE
PICTURE

A Family Hunt For An Unknown Man.

BY
MAGDEL ROETS

PUBLICATION
CONSULTANTS
We Believe In The Power Of Authors

PO Box 221974 Anchorage, Alaska 99522-1974
books@publicationconsultants.com,
www.publicationconsultants.com

ISBN Number: 978-1-59433-697-3
eBook ISBN Number: 978-1-59433-698-0

Library of Congress Catalog Card Number: 2017937567

Manufactured in the United States of America

Table of Contents

Chapter 1

Mystery of the Picture

"No, no, it can't be true! She can't be dead" exclaimed the shrivelled old woman.

"Sorry Aunt Johanna, I'm afraid it is true. Janneke passed away in her sleep," the matron of the old age home said soothingly. She took her by the arm and steered her back to her own room.

"But I saw her sleeping just ten minutes ago. Wanted to get her for breakfast, but she was still in bed. So I left her and went to the dining room alone."

"Maybe, but now she is no longer with us. Please excuse me now, Aunt Johanna, there are things I need to attend to." The matron walked briskly down the passage to her office, leaving poor old Johanna, bent at the waist, leaning hard on her walking stick, with a mixture of unbelief and sorrow. Her best and only friend was no more.

****

They found her with her hand on her heart. In her hand was a photograph. It was in black and white. It was old, very old. Maybe almost as old as Janneke herself. Time and much handling made the image look faded in places. It must have been touched often.

In the photo were several faces. It was a group photo of about twenty or more people. The face in the back row, third from the right was encircled in red. Daniel took the picture from his sister's hand to have a closer look. Who are these men in this old picture he wondered. Who was the man in the red circle? The same question was reflected in Sharon's eyes when he handed the photo back to her.

Together Sharon and Daniel went through the rest of Janneke's meagre possessions, hoping to find a clue as to who the man in the picture might be. Or might have been. He might not be alive anymore, Janneke herself having reached the age of eighty four. A sudden burst of moist filled Sharon's eyes. If only she had spent more time with her grandmother. If only she talked to her more and listened more.

"We know so little about her. It saddens me to realize we could have known her better, but we were always too busy to really sit down and listen to her." Daniel nodded, giving voice to his own thoughts: "Yeah, and now it's too late. Now we sit with this mystery and no one to answer our questions. Poor Grandma. Dying alone in a strange place away from her people." Daniel's words surprised his sister. He was not normally emotional, but their grandmother's death seemed to have touched him in a strange way. This made her lips tremble and tears running down her cheeks. She sniffed and put the photograph back in the painted tin the matron of the old age home gave her together with Janneke's other possessions. She poured them each another cup of coffee.

"Thanks for coming with me, Daniel. I could have done it myself; I know you're a busy man, but your support means a lot to me."

"No problem, Sis, you know at some point we both were quite close to Gran. It was the least I could do. I'll take care of all the funeral arrangements for you if you want me to. Or we could do it together."

"Together. I'd like that, yes." Sharon thought with longing in her heart, how good it is to have a brother to stand in for the absent husband.

"Do you think Merrill and Aunt Debby will come?" she asked.

"You're closer to them than me. Let them know about the arrangements as soon as everything is organized."

"I believe Aunt Debby's health is troubling, but I'd like to speak to her. Maybe she can shed some light on the photograph."

"Yes, you never know. She's a lot older than Mom was. Maybe she knows something about Gran's past."

"If only Mom and Dad were still here." Daniel nodded and emptied his cup.

"I have to get going now, but I'll start the arrangements as soon as I'm back at the office. I'll come by again tonight and we can discuss the details. In the meantime you can notify everyone that does not know yet."

"I'll get on it right away," Sharon said, tears welling up in her eyes again.

****

Sharon Hardy sat down at her kitchen table again after her brother, Daniel Moore had left. She took the photograph out of the tin box once more. Who was this man? Was it a relative; a friend, someone she loved? The picture was so old and faded; it was hard to make out the facial features. Yet it was clear that he had a strong jawline, friendly eyes and a mouth that could easily turn into a smile. Deep in thought was where Jacqui found her mother when she came home from school.

"Hi Mom, you home already? What's that you got there?" Sharon showed her daughter the picture.

"They found this in Great-gran's hand. She died with this photo in her hand, on her heart."

"Who's this guy circled in red?"

"No idea. But I'll not leave a stone unturned till I've found out."

"Cool. I'll help you. Just give me a clue and I'll Google till we get him. I'm sure it was Great-gran's first love. Somehow she lost him and after her hubs had died, she started thinking of him again."

"Slow down, girl. Maybe it's something completely different. Maybe it was a relative."

"Yeah. Right. Mom, you don't die with the picture of a relative on your heart."

"If it was a brother or her father, or someone close, it just might be enough reason to keep the picture close to your heart in your last moments."

"Yeah, well I don't know about brothers and fathers and stuff. All I know is that it's super romantic. Poor Great-gran. Suppose the guy broke her heart, but she kept on loving him. And poor Great-grandad didn't even know about it. Or ... how do you know it isn't

Great-grandad himself? Did you know him? How old were you when he died?"

"It's definitely not him. He had dark hair and dark brown eyes. Just like you. Look. This man had blond hair and bright eyes, blue or green or even grey."

"Just like her."

"Yes, just like her." Jacqui noticed the moist in her mother's eyes. She walked over to her and hugged her, saying: "Mom, I'm sorry. Here I carry on about romance, forgetting about how you feel. How do you feel? You'll miss her, won't you?"

"Yes. I'll miss her and I'm so sorry that I didn't spend more time with her. Didn't let you get to know her better. I was planning to go and see her next week. When the Home called this morning with the news that she had passed I felt cheated." Just like I felt cheated that Saturday morning when I bought a new toy for Snappy only to find him lying in the street, having been run over, Jacqui thought, only ten times worse, I guess, but she did not say anything. She just hugged Sharon once more and switched on the kettle to make some fresh coffee for her mother before she poured herself a glass of juice.

****

It was a small, quiet funeral. Daniel and Sharon, their families, their aunt Debby, cousin Merrill, the matron of the old age home and a few friends attended. Afterward the matron of the home offered refreshments. Sharon sat down next to her aunt with a cup of tea and a few tiny sandwiches.

"Aunt Debby, how much do you know about Gran's past? I mean, where she grew up, siblings, her parents and so on."

"I don't know a lot, she was very reserved, as you know. Never talked much about her past. All I know is that she was born in Rotterdam, in the Netherlands. They had to flee the Nazis, the family was split and she came to South-Africa with her mother."

"Flee from the Nazis? Were they Jewish?"

"No, Rotterdam was attacked early in the war. Many people fled, to England, I think. She and her mother managed to escape, but I believe her father was among a few hundred people who were killed."

"No brothers or sisters?"

"I think she had a brother. He was presumably killed with their father during the escape."

"And this is all you know?"

"Yes. I'm afraid that's all I know."

"How old was she when they left the Netherlands?"

"She was about four, I think. When they escaped, they were loaded on a ship and came directly here. They stayed in Cape Town for a while, then, I believe, her mother, my grandmother, remarried and moved to Johannesburg."

"What about boyfriends? Was Grandad her first love, or was there someone else in her past?"

"I have no idea. Why do you ask? I presume Granddad was her first love. She was so young when she married him." Sharon told her about the photograph found in her grandmother's hand after she had died. She promised to show her the picture someday. They talked some more and Sharon moved away to mingle.

An elderly lady approached her and introduced herself as Johanna.

"You know, I knew your grandma well." She nodded as she whispered loudly as if she was generously dispersing classified information.

"I live two doors from her." She held up two gnarled fingers. The importance of this had to sink in. Sharon had to know: just two doors, which meant Johanna practically, knew everything there was to know about Grandma Janneke. She nodded again to confirm.

"We were best friends, Janneke and I." Another nod and Sharon had to be sure all secrets could be revealed by the one and only Johanna.

"That's good to know, Johanna. I'm glad Gran had good friends. I'm sure she appreciated you." Sharon looked up to see if rescue was in sight when she caught the matron's eye who smiled and moved hear head left and right slightly, indicating poor Johanna could not be taken seriously.

"Johanna, it was nice to meet you. We'll talk some more later on. Will you please excuse me? There is someone I need to talk to also."

"Right, but come back to me. I want to tell you something." Sharon waved and turned away, Johanna already forgotten. She went on to speak to the matron to find out if there was new information about the photograph and the matron told her no, there was not. She went further from person to person enquiring subtly, but with no luck. People just carried on about how they loved Janneke and how much they'll miss her. It was a sad, but also dissatisfying gathering and Sharon dreaded it, wanting to go home first, politeness requiring that she stay till things fizzed out.

"So, Mom, Great-gran's funeral is done. Are you sad?"

"I'll miss her very much. I wonder how Gran would have handled it. They were close. And now it is only Uncle Daniel and me. No one else except for a few cousins scattered all over. People I hardly know."

"And none of them bothered to attend the funeral, except Aunt Debby and Aunty Merrill."

"Yes, what a shame. Families are no longer concerned or connected like when I was a child. If someone died, the whole family used to go, brothers, sisters, aunts and uncles, cousins, even second cousins could be expected."

"And I'm sure someone would know something about the picture."

"I asked Matron. She told me she asked around, but no one knows anything. There was this funny old lady, what's her name again? Oh, yes, Johanna. She seemed a bit disorientated. Even a bit, you know, not all there. She cornered me as if she had classified information to download on me. A bit paranoid if you ask me."

"Was that the one with the bright floral dress?"

"That's the one."

"What did she have to say? Did you ask her about the picture?"

"She didn't seem to know what was going on around her. I didn't think it was worth my time talking to her. And the matron insinuated that I do not take the old girl seriously."

"You never know. She might know more that we think. Maybe she really has something worthwhile to tell. If she were Geegee's best friend, she just might be the one who knows about the picture."

"Geegee?"

"Great-gran is such a long word. Can't I call her Geegee? It will save so much time."

"Sure you can call her Geegee. And great gran is not one word. It's two, or perhaps it's hyphenated."

"Whatever. But I think you must talk to 'Lady Floral dress'. She might surprize you."

"You read too many mystery stories."

"Mom! What harm can it do? Just talk to her. Besides, she seems lonely. Even if you don't get info from her, you will be doing a good deed and make her feel important."

"Oh, you. All right. I'll talk to her when I go again. There is one matter I need to finalize with the admin of the Home. I'll go early next week."

"Go in the afternoon so I can go with you."

"You, go to an old age home?"

"Yes, Mom, I like old people. They're not pretentious."

"Right. They have nothing to pretentious about. No longer a need to have to prove themselves or impress people; 'take me as I am or leave me.' Is that what you mean?"

"Exactly. 'take me or leave me, coz what you see is what you get'. Sometimes I wish everybody was like that."

Chapter 2

Starting the Search

It was long past midnight when Daniel found what he was looking for. Type one word on Google and you get a million distractions. He could have finished his search early, but for the distractions. From old, dollied up nature pictures, to purdah fashions, he took a tour through a magnitude of websites dealing with all kinds of photographic matters. He found a website that deals with identification, classification and dating of photos as old as sixty years and more. Quite excited, he sent an email explaining his problem, hoping to solve at least a part of the mystery of his grandmother's picture.

Early in the morning he was out of bed, careful not to disturb his wife Margot, who had been very patient and supportive. After a quick shower he went to the kitchen, got the coffee maker going and sat down at the table with his cell phone.

"Morning, Lazybones, are you up, or are you waiting for the sun to catch you in bed?"

"Daniel, goodness me," Sharon said, "what time is it? I've been working since three 'o clock. What are you up to this early?"

"Been Googling last night. I found a website that may be able to shed some light on our mystery picture."

"Uh, you too. Trying at all hours to find help and get a clue. Tell me what you found." He told his sister in detail how he went through about every site that dealt with photography and eventually sent an email to the one he opened just as he was about to call it quits. He promised to forward to her the reply as soon as he got it.

"Mom, who called so early?" Jacqui was standing behind her with a cup of fresh coffee.

"It's your Uncle Daniel. He found a website that might be able to give information on Geegee's picture. Thanks for the coffee. Just what I need right now." Sipping carefully the glorious hot liquid, holding the cup with both hands, she looked at her daughter.

"Where's yours?"

"That was actually mine. But don't worry. Enjoy. I'll get myself another cup. So, what does Uncle Daniel want?"

"He found a website that deals with old pictures. He thinks they might be able to help."

"Great. I hope they can ID everyone in that picture."

"I doubt if they can do that. They don't have a databank on every living person. All they might be able to do, is tell us when and maybe where it was taken, by what sort of camera, where it was developed and by what procedure and so on."

"What would that accomplish?"

"Well, we can go to the place where it was taken, try to find the same kind of camera or trace the developer. You never know where a lead may take us."

"And if we find the camera, we might find the owner, who knew the people?"

"I really don't know what we might be able to find. But it is a start and I will not stop until every possible lead has been followed and every clue been investigated.

"Cool. What's for breakfast?"

"Cereal and fruit. Help yourself, I have to be at the office early, so that I can leave early."

"Remember to pick me up when you go to the old age home. Why don't you work from home? You're the boss."

"There are documents I need. And I want to keep my staff on their toes."

"Just don't forget me."

"Will do. And now I need a warm shower urgently."

****

"Thank you for coming in, Mrs Hardy. It was a pleasure to take care of your grandmother. She was one of the nice ones. Some of the old folk are quite a handful."

"I can imagine. Thank you for taking so good care of her. I know she was happy here. Is everything settled now? Anything else I can be of assistance with, or needs my attention?"

"No, everything is in order. But you can come visiting your gran's friends anytime you like."

"Thank you. I just might do that. Now, let me collect my daughter and we'll be off. Thanks again." Sharon left the matron's office in search for Jacqui. She was nowhere in the building. Under a shade tree in the garden, Sharon spotted a young teenage girl sitting on a bench with an old woman dressed in a bright floral dress, waving around a walking stick. Walking over the lawn in their direction, she realized that they were in serious conversation. So much that they did not see her before she was standing right next to them.

"Hi Mom. Aunty Johanna and I are having a nice chat. And you won't believe what I have learned. Aunty Johanna, I think you met my mom before."

"Yes dear, I did. Hello Mrs. Hardy, how are you?"

"Very well, thank you, and you?"

"I'm well thanks for asking. I'm always well. You have a very special daughter."

"Thanks. I know. And she is very curious. I hope she hasn't tired you."

"Not at all, dear. It is so good to speak to a youngster who shows respect to elders. It is so scarce these days."

"Yes. Well, if the two of you are done ... "

"Tell your mother everything I told you today. And if you like, you can come visiting again. I'd like that."

"It's a promise, Aunty Johanna. See ya soon."

"Good bye, Jacqui, Mrs. Hardy."

"Good bye, Aunt Johanna".

Jacqui could hardly contain herself on the way home. She was so excited, wanting to tell what she had found out. But of course, she had to keep quiet and let her mother concentrate on the late afternoon traffic, which was heavy as usual.

At home she jumped out of the car, unlocked the front door, switched on the kettle for coffee and waited for her mother to appear from the garage where she secured the car before going in to the house. In the kitchen she found two cups of coffee ready and Jacqui sitting by the kitchen table hard at work on her cell phone.

"Jacqui, have your coffee and then get on with your homework."

"Mom, I'm hungry. Won't you please make me something, then I can tell you all the news Aunty Johanna told me."

"Nice try. It is less than ninety minutes to supper. You can snack on fruit. Start your homework and we can talk over supper. Go on."

"Mom! You can be so infuriating."

"I know. And someday you'll thank me. Now go!" If Sharon thought her daughter was planning to do homework of any kind before she had a chance to spill her beans, she was mistaken. But she didn't think so. Still, she had to try. Since she was a single parent, she had to maintain a level of discipline and was adamant not to neglect that responsibility. No exceptions. The routine will stay the same.

Jacqui sat on her bed, legs crossed, books open in front of her, cell phone next to her, beckoning. She tried her utmost to ignore the little electronic device. It was a battle which she lost after an eternity of thirty seconds. Book in one hand, phone in the other, she started logging in to Facebook. It took a few attempts to find the person she was looking for, the person Aunty Johanna told her about. She sent a friend request and waited, one eye on the screen, the other on the book in her hand.

Jacqui actually managed to retrieve a pen and exercise book from her school case before the screen lit up and the friend request was answered. Time to do some serious research now. School books completely forgotten.

Chapter 3

Rotterdam under Attack

The afternoon of 14th May 1940. Most people had fled the inner city of Rotterdam. Bombarding of the other Dutch cities for four days sent them out south to seek safety and shelter away from the strategic targets of the German bombers. An attack was expected, therefore the number of casualties - just under one thousand - was relatively low, in spite of allied media reports of the barbaric deeds of destruction by the enemy, resulting in 'almost thirty thousand civilian deaths'. But whoever got caught between the bombs dropping from the Stukas in the sky and the flamethrowers on the ground, there was little chance of escape.

The Rotterdam Blitz was so successful, having flattened the city in record time, the Dutch government capitulated. But it did take a threat of doing the same to the city of Utrecht before General Winkelman surrendered at the small town of Rijsoord on the south eastern side of Rotterdam.*

Hans Verbeek tried to keep his family together and safe, not believing the attack will reach their part of town. But it did. Their house was not directly hit. Shrapnel from the building across the street, that took a direct hit, almost destroyed the front of their house. They were hiding back in the kitchen when a neighbour hammered on the backdoor, shouting and beckoning them to follow him. There were soldiers who were trying to get people out of the area and they knew a safe route. Hans grabbed his son's hand and shouted to his wife to bring their daughter. He waited for her to leave the house first.

Suddenly a flamethrower appeared round the corner, some shooting took place, people screamed and fell in the crossfire. Hanna, Hans's wife got frightened, ducked back into the house, her daughter clutched in her arms. In the confusion Hans lost track of her. Yelling over the cacophony, not hearing another sound but burning rubble, explosions all around and people screaming in agony, he could not determine through the smoke and dust where his wife and daughter were.

The bombs started falling again, leaving buildings in burning ruins. Desperately he looked around for his family, but the smoke was thick and suffocating. Turning around, he saw what was left of his house, was nothing but rubble. No, no! They couldn't be in there. A soldier grabbed his arm and dragged him away, not realising the bundle Hans held close to his chest was his little boy. They were bundled into a military vehicle with seven other civilians and driven away.

The soldiers assured him no one could have survived the attack and how lucky they were. In the back of his mind he asked himself if he could survive, why not his wife and daughter too? But the evidence against it was overwhelming. He saw with his own eyes his collapsed house and all the chaos around it. How could anyone come out of that?

****

Hans Verbeek took his little son's hand in his. Vicus tried to pull away, but Hans held firm, talking softly, gently to the boy:

"Kom je maar mee, jonge. Wij moeten op de schip gaan. Hier sijn wij niet meer veijlig." The boy followed him reluctantly, scared of the big ship and all the people rushing in all directions. When they at last found a place on the deck to sit down, Hans took a couple of bread rolls from a bag and, holding his son close to his body, handed him a roll. The boy took the roll, took a small bite, chewed and swallowed. Then he looked up into his father's face. With big, worried eyes, he said:

"Waar sijn Moeder en Janneke? Wanneer gaan hulle op de schip klimmen?"

"Vicus, jonge, dat weet ik niet". Hans turned his head away so that the boy could not see the tears streaming down his cheeks. Never, Vicus, he thought, they are never going to get on the ship. They are dead, blown to pieces by German bombs. If only they could get away earlier. If only they were not separated in the cross fire. Then maybe he could have protected them. O, Here, wat een beproefing. He prayed softly into the wind, so that the boy would not hear him.

Arriving in London, they were taken to a place prepared for refugees from Holland. There were already a number of people. Several families opened their houses to strangers. Some houses were already filled, many were still taking people in, filling every available space. Hans and his four year old son were taken in by John and Amy Anderson where they shared a bedroom with two other men. They were allowed to refresh and then invited into the dining room for a hearty meal, the first proper meal in days.

A routine was quickly established. Hans would take his boy after lunch and go to the docks to see if, by some miracle his wife and daughter survived and made it on another ship to Brittan. Day after day they watched, waited and went home at dusk, sad and disappointed.

The weather was sunny some days, other days, unpleasant, wind blowing away everything it could pick up. Vicus held on to his hat for dear life, but the wind caught it at a moment he lost focus. He ran after it, and as he was about to grab it, the wind caught it again and took it further away. Hans ducked and dived to avoid knocking people over to keep up and not lose track of his son. He could get lost among the crowds easily, never to be found by anyone familiar. In spite of the weather, the man and his son were seen every day, waiting, watching.

But Hans would not give up and Vicus would not let him. Until that day the boy could not take it anymore. As they were about to turn around and go home, the boy sat down, holding on to Hans' leg and started sobbing. He told Hans he did not want to do it anymore. He could not come to the docks every day looking and every day not seeing his mother and twin sister. He begged Hans to stop coming.

The people in the house where he lived also discouraged him to go to the docks every day. If his family had survived, they would have made it by now. His flame of hope died and so did he. He breathed, ate, talked, slept, woke up, but he merely existed. He did not live anymore. When London was attacked, he sent Vicus with many other children to live in the country where they would be safe. Hans helped his hosts wherever he could, helped them build their bomb shelter in the small backyard, helped other refugees in many ways and made himself as useful as his strength allowed.

When time allowed, he wrote letters to his son. He also made contact through an old friend from Rotterdam, Frederik van Halsten, who fled and arrived in London a day before him, with a man who could get letters into Holland and back. Hans gave him letters to send to his cousin in Amsterdam. Of course there were never guarantees that the letters would reach their destiny, but people kept on trying. After several months, Hans got a letter from his cousin. But the news was not good. His cousin had had no word of his wife and daughter, the death of his brother and two sisters was confirmed, half of his own family was wiped out, he and all who survived was about to leave Holland for America.

It was believed that all German spies had left England before the war broke out. Even the historians, years later, confirmed that. However, there were a few people in intelligence who thought otherwise. They believed they identified at least three foreigners posing as refugees, trying to infiltrate British society. According to their information, these men and one woman were part of an operation that would get close to a certain general with connections in the war office. One of the intelligence officers was a family friend of Frederik von Halsten whose father did business with Frederik's father years ago. Frederik, known to be trustworthy, was recruited in an operation to find any information about the spies and give it through to the handler.

Frederik convinced Hans to take part in this underground operation involving the identification and exposure of German spies, who were believed to be infiltrating all levels of British society. Since Hans could speak German well, he would be of great help, especially because he was alone and free to move around. Frederik himself still had his wife to take care of, although she was determent to get involved in their covert operation. Their little girl, Annika, almost three years older that Vicus, was also sent to live in a country town. It was a pity Vicus and Annika were not placed together. They would have been a great comfort to each other. Hans got Annika's address and encouraged Vicus to write to her. In better times, Annika was the twins', Vicus and Janneke's best friend.

Frederik took Hans with him to the docks to see if they could perhaps spot a German spy among the people coming and going. They knew who they were looking for and kept their eyes focused. At first it was difficult, remembering his little boy's disappointment went they went looking for their loved ones. After a while he got used to it and caught himself looking at the throngs moving around like ants, but never expecting to see a familiar face. Then he would go about his business of spy hunting again.

Together they identified two more of the most wanted Germans posing as refugees. Their plans to trap them in secret and eliminate them succeeded only partially. Hans never liked killing anything. He did not hunt, he was not a killer at heart. War changes everything. When he got the order to kill the Germans, he hesitated and acted a split second too late. One was dead before he hit the ground, the other was fatally wounded, but managed to get away. He reached a rendezvous point and warned his commander seconds before he drew his last breath. In a revenge attack Hans was killed, but the cell of Germans had to break up temporarily as more were now identified and their rendezvous point revealed.

****

After the war Vicus was taken in by Frederick and his wife for a while. He was by now a big boy who understood death and realised he was alone. His well doer's health deteriorated because of several war wounds and he died a few years later. Vicus went back to Holland after finishing his studies in engineering. Proud of his accomplishments, he sent Annika a photo of him with his final year classmates. He married and with correspondence between them waning, he almost lost contact with Annika.

He had a son they named Gerhard. His wife, Kate was heartbroken about the many war orphans and convinced Vicus to foster whenever a child needed a temporary home. One child, Stephen Farlow was older than most of the babies they fostered. All the little ones got adopted, but Stephen was too old. Everyone always wanted babies, Stephen was already past his toddler years. When they realized the Farlow boy had nowhere else to go, they adopted him to be a big brother for their little Gerhard. Kate died young of asthma and he took his sons to the land of sunshine and opportunity, South Africa.

Landing in the Cape during wet and cold winter weather Vicus decided not to stay in Cape Town, but move around. Everybody told him the best opportunities for work are in the Transvaal, especially Johannesburg. He was about to pack up and go there when a fellow refugee came knocking one day and told him about a friend who had work for a couple of men in Durban. It was at an engineering plant and could use the kind of expertise Vicus had to offer. That was a certainty and Vicus did not hesitate. In his last letter to Annika, he told her about this job at a big harbour in South Africa. When her reply came, he was gone without leaving a forwarding address. He got busy and never wrote again.

He worked hard while a widowed neighbour, Trudy, looked after the boys Gerhard and Stephen. She was a gentle, soft spoken person, intelligent and resourceful. The boys were happy to stay with her during the day. Her son Jonathan, about the same age as Stephen, became their best friend. Vicus and Trudy spent more time together as time passed. It was quite convenient that they fell in love. In spite of the age difference, Trudy was almost five years older than Vicus, they married and Vicus adopted Jonathan as his own. One happy family, not without a squabble once in a while, but overall content and functioning well.

The childhood memories of his mother and twin sister, Janneke, dying in Rotterdam never completely left him, but grew vague and retreated into the back of his mind to make space for his new life with his new family.

Chapter 4

Janneke

The little girl held on to her mother's hand for dear life. The hundreds of people milling about scared her, believing that if she got lost, her mother would never find her. Having already lost her father and brother, she didn't want to be separated from her mother even for a minute. She was still longing for them and hoping they would find them somewhere. On the busy docks of the London harbour it seemed likely, especially for a four year old.

Hanna and her daughter weaved through the throngs of people. They just managed to keep up with their guide who led them from the ship that brought them from Holland, to the one going to South Africa. Suddenly she froze in her tracks. That man there, she thought. Could it be? Hans! She wanted to shout, but what if it was not him? There he was again, looking around as if he was trying to find someone in the crowds. He looked so much like her Hans! Her guide urged her on and she lost sight of the man who was obviously looking for someone.

"Hans!" She shouted out as loud as her voice allowed her. "Hans, Hans!" The next moment he turned aside and started running in the opposite direction as if he was chasing after something, or someone. Then he disappeared among the crowds. Her heart sank down to her shoes. She turned and, holding her daughter's hand even tighter, she followed her guide, who was getting impatient. The ship was about to leave the harbour and if they wanted to catch it, they'd have to hurry. The next boat wouldn't leave within a week.

The voyage down south was mostly uneventful. That allowed lots of time for Hanna to think. And wonder. About the man on the docks. Was it Hans? What if it were Hans? He might think they died in Rotterdam. Just like they have assumed until now, that he died in Rotterdam. What if, what if, what if?

But it was not possible. She tried in vain to convince herself it could not have been Hans. Hans and Vicus could not have survived the bomb attack that day. They were outside. She saw the flamethrower, the renewed bombing attack, heard the crossfire and everything going up in flames all around. How could anyone survive that? The only reason she and Janneke survived, was because they were still inside the house, which was badly damaged, but provided enough shelter to protect them. That was the reason they survived. How could Hans and Vicus possibly have survived such a brutal bombing? Minutes later her own house was almost flattened. If it were not for the soldiers that came in from the front and carried them out, they would have been blown to pieces in an instant.

She didn't want to leave; she wanted to search for her family; her husband and her little boy. Having no patience, the soldiers literally carried her and her daughter to a waiting military vehicle a hundred meters away. There were two other women already inside, sobbing. Another man with a badly injured leg was dragged into the truck and then they drove off south. They spent the night at a house with some other refugees. The next day they were sneaked out to another house and from there they were taken to a ship that took them to Brittan where they would catch a boat to South Africa if they so preferred. It was highly recommended.

And then she saw the man on the dock. He looked so much like Hans. Or did she want to see him so badly that her imagination took over? No, the man on the docks could not have been Hans. He just looked like him. Still, she was only ninety nine percent convinced her husband and son were dead. That one percent possibility would always be in the back of her mind. What if.

****

Stepping down on solid soil after many, many days on the water was almost like being freed from jail. Since the big, flat mountain appeared on the horizon, they have been watching it growing bigger as they got closer to land. They have never seen anything like it before. From the flat planes of the Netherlands, to this enormous rock soaring into the clouds took some getting used to. They were still a mile or two out at sea when the sun broke through the clouds one morning. The mountain stood in all its majesty in front of them. Soon after, the clouds closed in again and pouring rain drove everyone below deck.

To all the Dutch refugees, this weather was quite normal. It was the hot, dry summer that was hard for them to endure. Hanna Verbeek and her little girl were taken in by a family from German decent. Since Hanna could speak a little German and her hosts spoke a little Dutch, they could communicate at some level. They would sometimes try to get Afrikaans and Dutch together, and that did not go so badly. Afrikaans was after all a daughter language of Dutch and there were numerous similarities where they could connect. In fact, Hanna insisted they teach her Afrikaans as it was the language of the land and she intended to fully integrate.

She refused to be a burden and did her part of the house work. From time to time there were opportunities to earn a few Pounds and she fully made use of it to pay for her keep. Everyone struggled to make ends meet during the war years and Hanna would not hear of taking anything for nothing. When she could not find paid employment, she helped her hosts by making a small vegetable garden in their back yard. Having one's own food ready for the picking was a great help.

After the war ended, things changed rapidly for all people, including for Hanna and her little girl, Janneke. Her host's brother came visiting from Johannesburg, fell in love with Hanna, married her and took his new family back with him to Johannesburg. Janneke grew up there, got a good education and married a lawyer who lost all he possessed on the stock market. They had three children, Debby, Nanette and James. Debby struggled with poor health most of her adult life. She had one daughter, Merrill. James emigrated to Canada and was seldom heard of afterward.

Nanette had two children, Daniel and Sharon. Nanette was married to Chris, a wealthy businessman whose favourite pass time was flying around in his own little Beechcraft. Daniel and Sharon were both young adults pursuing their careers, when their parents' little aeroplane went missing one Saturday somewhere in the Drakensberg mountain range. It was found the next day scattered over a grassy patch north of Ladysmith in Natal. Janneke was shattered. The event caused her grandchildren, Daniel and Sharon to grow closer to her. They were a great comfort, while she tried to fill the gap for them left by the death of their parents.

Chapter 5

Friends on Facebook

Mary Cork answered the friend request from Helena Nel from Nijmegen in Holland. She found her name in a gardening group they both belonged to. A comment by Mary about managing garden slugs attracted Helena's attention. She wanted to know more and after a number of conversations, Helena decided to send Mary a friend request.

Slowly they got to know each other better. Occasionally they exchanged information about their personal lives, environment, friends, family. They both had grandmothers still alive. Mary's grandmother lived in an old age home, Helena's lived with a cousin, Grieta, in Maastricht.

Grieta's grandparents on her father's side were also still alive, nearing their nineties, but healthy and all their faculties intact. They were originally from Rotterdam. They fled to England during World War Two and never returned until their children went back. Not wanting to leave their aging parents alone in Brittan, the children convinced them to come and live with them back in the fatherland. Now Annika and her British husband were living with their loving granddaughter Grieta and her generous husband, Karel, in a big house on the outskirts of Maastricht.

Mary told Helena that one of her Grandmother's friends in the old age home was also from Holland, originally. Her grandmother, Johanna talked a lot to this friend and the friend, Aunt Janneke told many stories from her early childhood in Rotterdam. Some memories from her time in Rotterdam were more vivid than yesterday's breakfast.

Once more Helena was intrigued. She told Grieta everything Mary told her. Grieta told her grandmother's friend, Annika, the story about Cousin Helena's friend, Mary, whose grandmother, Janneke was from Rotterdam and all the experiences she could still recall after so many years. Although her health was deteriorating, according to Mary, her mind was bright and her memory clear.

At the same time Mary told her grandma, Johanna, everything she had learned from her Facebook friend, Helena in Nijmegen. On a visit to Johanna, Mary was taken to Janneke's room and told her the things she had shared with her gran. It was when she mentioned the name of Grieta's gran in Maastricht, that Janneke's eyes lit up as if a light was switched on in her brain.

"What did you say your friend Grieta's grandmother's name was?"

"Annika. Her grandma's name is Annika."

"I knew a girl named Annika. In Rotterdam. We were best friends. She was a few years older than us, but we were best friends."

"Us, you mean ... ?"

"I had a brother."

"Janneke, we have known each other so many years and you have never told me about your brother."

"There is not much to tell. He's dead. He died with my father in the Rotterdam Blitz. He was my twin brother." The last words came out as a whisper from quivering lips. When no one found words to say, she continued:

"My father waited too long to evacuate. We were caught in the bombing. My mother and I got separated from them. We survived and they were killed. When there was a short break in the bombing, some soldiers grabbed us and brought us to safety. From there we were taken by ship to England, then onto another ship to South Africa. We stayed in Cape Town until the war ended. My mother remarried and we came to live with my stepfather here in Johannesburg. I missed them so much. I never forgot my brother. Never will. Still wondering how it would have been if I hadn't lost him. His name was Vicus.

And so the story told by Janneke to Johanna and her granddaughter found its way via Facebook back to Maastricht, through Helena who told Grieta, who told Annika. Annika felt a break down coming on when she heard the story. She had to lie down and be revived with a small tot of brandy. Half an hour later, Grieta had to repeat the story. She approached her grandmother carefully, not to shock the old woman into her grave.

"Are you sure that's what she said? Her name is Janneke and her twin brother is Vicus?"

"Yes, granny, I can check if you like. I can ask Helena to make sure. But I'm pretty sure that's what she said."

"Ik kan't niet gloven, Grietje." Annika always called her Grietje when a situation was delicate.

"Grietje, my child, I can't believe this. All, these years I have believed Janneke and her mother were dead, killed in the bombardment of the city. I cried with Vicus over the death of his little sister. And now I don't even know if he is still alive. We have corresponded for years after the war. Later he emigrated. His wife had died and I learned that he wanted to leave the bad memories behind. He took his young sons, I think their names were Gerhard and Stephan, and went to South Africa. They both went to South Africa each believing the other had died. Just imagine that. If only he kept in contact with me. I could have brought them together. You must phone Janneke. I want to speak to her. I must tell her the good news about her brother. But maybe you should break the news gently first or she might need more than a tot of brandy.

During the next few minutes the Facebook lines got red hot with the news Annika had told Grieta. Grieta told Helena, who told Mary. Mary drove to the old age home and told Johanna who, very gently and very subtly brought the news to Janneke that her childhood friend Annika wanted to speak to her about her twin brother, Vicus. It was decided that Annika would be the one to break the news that Vicus survived and was living in South Africa.

Chapter 6

Phone Reunion

"Annika, is it really you?"

"It is really me, Janneke. You'll never know how overjoyed I was when I learned that you were alive." They both cried a little, the emotion of the moment too great to be contained in language. When they started talking again, there was so much to say, to ask, that they both talked at the same time, stopped to give the other a chance to say something, and then they would both start talking again at the same moment.

"I still have letters he wrote me, Janneke. For some reason I could never get myself to get rid of them. I even have a photograph he sent me shortly after finishing his studies."

"You don't! Do you? What did he look like when he was grown up?"

"Oh, he was quite handsome. You'd be so proud. Say, why don't I send you the picture?"

"You can't do that. You can't let go of a souvenir as precious as that."

"Perhaps, Janneke," Annika said slowly, contemplatively, "you are the reason I could not let go of those letters and the picture. Perhaps you need them more that I do." Her decision was final. She was going to send at least the photograph to Janneke. It was her brother. Her twin brother. Janneke needed to have it. They talked some more and promised to stay in contact. After half an hour they were emotionally exhausted and said good bye.

****

Three days later a parcel was delivered at the old age home by way of overnight courier. With trembling fingers Janneke opened the parcel. One by one she took the letters in both hands and read them, tears streaming unrestrained down her cheeks. These were her brother's words, his handwriting, his pen and ink touched the paper. Perhaps there were even some of his fingerprints on the paper. Overcome by emotion when she looked at the picture and recognized his smile in the red encircled face of her brother, she put the letters in a neat heap next to her on the bed, took the picture in her hand, placed her hand on her heart and sobbed until she fell asleep. A sleep from which she would not wake up.

A light breeze blew in from the wide open window. The letters were picked up and scattered all over the floor. The cleaner came, saw the mess and cleared it up. She worked quietly not to disturb the sleeping old lady. All the papers scattered over the floor, were dumped in the trash with everything else that was not in place. When she left the room, all was neat and tidy as it should be.

****

Mary Cork checked her Facebook notifications to see if there was something from Helena. It was the hardest thing she ever had to do to call Helena with the news that Janneke died shortly after receiving the parcel from Grieta. Worst was the fact that the letters had disappeared. When Janneke died, the matron of the old age home found only the photo. No sign of the letters that accompanied the photo. According to Helena, Grieta's grandmother, Annika, took the news about Janneke's death badly. The joy of founding Janneke after so many years, was now overshadowed by her death. Shattered as she was, though, she insisted that Grieta do all she could to help find Vicus. It was too late to be reunited with his sister, but he should know she survived the war and was living in South Africa, maybe a stone's throw from where he lived.

There was nothing of significance from either Helena or Grieta, whom she also got to know on Facebook. There was a friend request. One from someone named Jacqui Hardy. Without investigating Jacqui's timeline, she accepted the request, then clicked back on home without giving her newest friend, Jacqui another thought. But Jacqui was not to be forgotten. She immediately received a response from her: 'Hi Mary, I'm Janneke's great granddaughter. Aunty Johanna at the old age home gave me your name and said you can help me with info on Janneke's background. Please help me if you can. My mom's driving me nuts.' Now this is interesting, thought Mary. But first find out more about this great granddaughter, she thought. She clicked on Jacqui's profile to see what kind of person she is. Perhaps a prankster or a hacker with evil intent.

The profile surprised her. Jacqui loved classical music almost as much as modern gospel music, Hillsongs being her favourite group. She was two years away from qualifying as a ballet teacher. What? At this age? She is not yet sixteen. She'll have to find out how this could be possible. Jacqui also loved animals but sadly no pets were allowed in the apartment building where she now lived. Her ambition was to become a marine biologist. Jacqui seemed to be a serious kind of girl. Probably an A-grade student. Still, Mary considered it necessary to investigate a little more before she gave any information to this young stranger. She clicked on message and into Jacqui's inbox she typed: 'Hi Jacqui, what exactly do you know already and what would you like to know?'

Immediately the response came: 'There was a picture in my great-gran's hand when she died. No idea where it came from, no idea who the people in it might be. If you know anything about it, please, please let me know.' Of course she knew everything about the picture. Better than to tell her, put her in contact with Helena and let it go from there: 'I know someone who might be able to help you. Go to my profile, to my friends, find Helena Smit and send her a friend request. That is the best I can do for now.' Better warn Helena:

'Hello Helena, something interesting just happened. Janneke's great granddaughter just contacted me. Her name is Jacqui Hardy. She wants information about that photograph Grieta sent to Janneke. I suggest you accept her Facebook friend request so you can communicate with her. She should talk to Grieta asap. And maybe to your gran, if possible. How is Annika? Coping alright? Let me know what happens'.

Before Mary's message came through, the notification from Jacqui's request appeared on Helena's cell phone screen. Uhg, not now, Helena thought and put the phone down again. I don't have time for Facebook right now. When Mary's message came through, she gave up and read it. Amazed, she accepted Jacqui's request. After a short exchange, she asked her cell phone number and promised to give it to the right person who will give her a call soon.

Within minutes, Jacqui's cell phone rang: "Daag, my name is Grieta. Am I speaking to Jacqui Hardy?"

"Hi Grieta, yes, I am Jacqui. Did Helena give you my number?"

"I just had an es-em-es from her. Are you really Janneke's great granddaughter?"

"I am. But tell me please, how do you know my great-gran and what can you tell me about her background?"

"Helena told me you found the picture I sent her? Do you still have it?"

"Have it?! My mom won't ever let go of it. It's like it's become her most prized possession. So, you're the one who sent it to my great gran? Tell me about it, please. Who are the people in that picture that was so important to my great gran that she died with it, holding it in her hand on her heart."

"The man that was encircled in red was her brother."

"Her brother? She had a brother?"

"Yes. A twin brother."

"Where is he now?"

"I don't exactly know. All I know is that he went to South Africa after his wife died here in Holland. I suppose he is still there, but I'm not sure. I'm not even sure if he is still alive."

"Well, exactly how do you know about him?"

"Janneke and Vicus, that is the name of her twin brother; they had a friend. That was before the war. Her name is Annika and she is my grandmother. She was in contact with him for many years after the war. He sent her that picture after he finished his studies. Later he got married and they had a son. His wife was sickly and died a few years later. That was when he decided to leave Holland. He got a job at some big harbour in South Africa and that was the last my gran heard from him."

"Wow, wow. I don't know what to say. Thank you so much for calling me so quickly. My mom will be thrilled to know all this."

"Why didn't your mom make all these inquiries?"

"Oh, she's trying her best to find info, she just looks in the wrong places. I stumbled on something and followed up on it. Almost by accident". She told Grieta how nobody took Aunty Johanna seriously and how she, on a visit to the home, started talking to her under a shade tree where she told her about her granddaughter, Mary who knew some people in Holland who knew my great grandmother."

"Very interesting. And isn't it wonderful what the social media can do for you? I'll tell my gran about our conversation and we'll talk some more. Perhaps I can let you and your mom talk to her. I know she'd love that. But I'll break the news gently first."

"Great. My mom with be over the roof if she knows. I better go and tell her right away. I think supper's ready anyway. Just pray she doesn't kill me first. I am supposed to be doing homework right now. But it was great talking to you, Grieta. Shall I call you Aunt Grieta? You must be a bit older than I?"

"I don't know. Just as long as you don't call me something ugly it doesn't really matter to me. Grieta is fine. Alright then, go tell your mom and make sure you do your homework before you go to bed. I'll talk to my gran and we'll call again sometime soon. Good night, then." Just then the call came from the kitchen:

"Jacqui! Supper is ready. Come to the table please."

"Be right there," she yelled back. As soon as she was seated, Sharon asked:

"Who have you been talking to? I heard your phone ringing, and I heard you talking for quite a while instead of doing homework. Would you care to enlighten me, young lady?"

"Mom, of course I'll tell you, but you need to sit down first. Sit down, say grace, dish up, then I'll tell you word for word the conversation I just had. It's amazing." Ignoring her daughter's "orders", Sharon went to the kitchen to fetch serviettes and condiments to put on the table before she settled down.

"Mom, did you know GeeGee had a brother?"

"My aunt Debby mentioned it at the funeral. Why, how do you know?" Then Jacqui started talking.

By the end of the meal, which was cold by the time they finally got around to eating it, Sharon was in awe and close to tears. If only Janneke could live until they have found her brother. She was not well and the shock of seeing her brother in a picture after so many years must have been too much to bear. Sharon was proud of her daughter for pursuing the matter until she found results.

Solving the problem of the identity of the man in the picture is a good thing. Finding answers to the million questions that arose from that was a new challenge: Where is this brother Vicus? Is he still alive? What about his family? Grieta said he had a son. Where is this son? How did Janneke and Vicus got separated? What about their parents? Where did they go, where did they die? Janneke's family never knew about the brother, except one. Debby knew about a brother. Did she know they were twins? She'll have to be told. We didn't know about Vicus, does Vicus or his family know about us? Probably not, Sharon thought.

While Jacqui stacked the dishes in the washer and tidied up, Sharon called her brother to find out what he had learned. Nothing much, he told her. He was stunned at the news Sharon had for him. He was tied up with work for the night, but promised to go over the next evening and then they would call Grieta in Holland. There must be more they can learn from her. Some clue as to the whereabouts of Vicus Verbeek.

Chapter 7

Doug Verbeek

The old man folded the newspaper just so, then placed it at the bottom of the cage.

"Newspaper, newspaper," the bird said, "dirty, dirty newspaper" He also added a few dirty words.

"Mind your language! Ek gaan jou nek omdraai, jou stupid voël."

"Stupid voël, stupid voël".

"Shut up and give me a kiss, stupid voël." The parrot jumped on the old man's shoulder and 'kissed' him on the cheek: "Kiss me, kiss me, kissssss meeee," said the bird: "Ek gaan jou nek omdraai, nek omdraai, kissss meee, ek gaan jou nek omdraaaaai." Suddenly the bird saw the neighbour's cat walking by on the lawn and started barking like a dog. The frightened cat made a u turn and disappeared behind a bush.

"Naughty cat, naughty cat."

"Yes, good boy, Polly, chase away the naughty cat."

"Good boy, Polly, good boy, gooood boooooy."

"Come on, Polly, it's time to go inside. It's getting windy out here on the patio". The old man rolled himself into the living room, pulling the bird cage that was mounted on wheels, and closed the patio door. In the kitchen he stuck a light meal in the microwave oven, set the table for one, place the bird's bowl on the other side of the table, then emptied the warmed up food onto his plate. He filled Polly's bowl with parrot food, thanked the Father and started eating while the bird walked over the table to start on his own supper.

Early the next morning the old man and his bird were back on the patio of his unit in the luxurious retirement village in the north of Durban. After a breakfast of Weet Bix, raw oats and mixed fruit yogurt, it was time to clean the cage again. The old man was very particular about the health and cleanliness of his beloved Polly. Like every morning he removed the soiled newspaper, folded a new one and put it just so, at the bottom of the cage. Every morning and every afternoon, without exception.

"You drop too much, you know that? Polly? I should stop feeding you," he said as he pulled the soiled newspaper out of the cage. He must ask Douggie for more old newspapers, or he'd be running out. Then his hand froze. His eyes widened, he shook his head, reading the words again and again: 17th October 1935. His own birthdate. Janneke ... Verbeek ... No! No! No! It cannot be! No! He wanted to scream, but no sound found its way out of his throat. It is a mistake, must be a mistake. He read the words again. They haven't change since he read it seconds ago. There in black and white it is in the obituary columns of the soiled newspaper, name and birthdate: 'Janneke Proctor, born Verbeek, 17th October 1935, died 12 January 2019'. How can this be, how is it possible? Janneke dead? Now? A month ago? She died with Mother in the bombing! How can she have survived that?

He relived that day. His father grabbed him and ran out of the house, screaming at his mother to bring Janneke and run. There was the sound of gunfire, bombs exploding, flames everywhere. He cried, his father kept on running, then stopped and looked back. The house where they lived was in ruins. His father wanted to turn back, but a soldier grabbed him, yelling for him to come quick or miss the opportunity to be rescued. How could she have survived? And what about Mother? Were they saved, was Janneke rescued by someone else? What exactly happened? A million questions churned his mind. He felt faint. He needed his medicine. The parrot somehow sensed his master's agony. He jumped onto his shoulder and rubbed his head against the old man's ear, making soft noises. The old man rolled himself into the bathroom, took a bottle of pills from the cabinet and swallowed two tablets that he washed down with tap water.

Back on the patio he read the words again, over and over. His sister died alone, not seven hundred kilometres from him. And he didn't know. If only ... The tears started streaming down his cheeks, ran through his beard and made puddles on his pants. His body trembled as the sobbing grew in intensity. The neighbour heard the noise and came to investigate. He just showed her the newspaper and kept on crying. Without a word she went into the house and pressed the panic button. This man needed help, and fast.

****

"Granddad, are you feeling better now? Do you want to tell me what happened?" Doug sat down next to his grandfather's bed, concern darkening his bright blue eyes.

"The newspaper. I was cleaning Polly's cage. When I took out the soiled paper I saw it. The obituary. My sister. She died. My sister is dead and I didn't even know she was alive."

"Your sister? You're not making sense, Granddad. She's dead, but you didn't know she was alive. I didn't even know you had a sister."

"Never talked about her. We thought she died in the war, the bombing of Rotterdam. My father and I escaped, but she was killed with my mother. Or so we thought. But there, in the obituaries is proof that she had made it out. She lived here on my doorstep and I didn't know it. She probably thought I was dead. Like I thought she was. I wonder if my mother made it out. But how? And now that she is really dead I can never ask her the million questions I now need answered."

"Wow, I'm so sorry. I didn't know all this. Shouldn't we try to trace her family? Where is the obituary? There should be some info we can use to trace them."

"That would be nice. See what you can do, will you? And now, Douggie boy, your granddad needs to rest. Those pills they gave me on top of the ones I took make me sleepy.

Will you please feed the bird and put him in his cage? Put the cage in the living room. We can talk tomorrow."

Doug Verbeek did as he was asked, but he didn't leave immediately. First he made a few phone calls asking around to find accommodation for his sons for the night. When he stroke luck, he quickly drove home, delivered his sons at a neighbour's house for the night, packed an overnight bag for himself and returned to his granddad's place. In concurrence with the administration of the retirement village it was decided that Vicus Verbeek should not spend the night alone. Frail care was available and the panic button was there, but Doug did not trust the people in charge after hearing horror stories from other residents. He would make sure his old guy was safe and if need be, take him home the next day. In the meantime, he would start making enquiries to see if he could trace the sister's family.

****

"Good morning. This is Doug Verbeek speaking. I'd like to speak to Mister Moore, Daniel Moore, please."

"Good morning, Doug, I'm Daniel. What can I do for you?"

"I found your name on the obituary of a certain Janneke Proctor. Is that correct? Are you the one who placed the notice in the paper?"

"I am. What did you say your name is?"

"It's Verbeek, Doug Verbeek. I believe I am related to Janneke. And I assume you are her grandson, according to the notice in the paper?"

"That is correct. In what way are you related? You have the same surname as her maiden name. Are you ... ?"

"Yes, I am the grandson of her brother Vicus." Daniel was silent for a moment, rubbing his chin. This is unbelievable, he thought.

"I've been trying to find him, Vicus, ever since we learned about his existence. We only found out after Granny died. How did you find me? You said something about an obituary, but she's been dead more than a month."

"Yes, and we almost missed it. My granddad, Vicus saw the notice in the paper when he cleaned his bird cage. He took the old, soiled newspaper from the bottom of the cage and only then he saw it. The poor old guy was overwhelmed and needed to be calmed because he thought she had died in the war when they were little."

"Yes, I can believe that. She probably thought he had died in the war. She never spoke about him or her experiences as a child. We found out about him when she died with a photograph in her hand. We traced the origin of the picture back to Holland and were told the man in the picture was her twin brother."

"Wow, this is unbelievable."

"My thoughts exactly. Listen, Doug, I need to go, but I'll contact you very soon. We have a lot to talk about. A million questions need answers. Say hi to your granddad for me and make sure he's okay. Can I call you tonight? Maybe I can talk to him also?"

"Sure. I'll be visiting him, so call any time after six."

****

Another phone reunion took place. Daniel called Doug on his cell phone at precisely ten minutes after six. They talked for a few minutes, then Doug gave the phone to his granddad so that he could speak to his late sister's grandson. It was an emotional conversation that caused the old man to shed tears all over again. When they have said good bye Doug wanted to give him a sedative again, but he declined.

"Not necessary, Son, I'm fine."

"Are you sure, Granddad, at your age you should not take chances ..."

"What do you mean, 'my age'? Am I old? Do I look old? I'm not old, I'm merely post-mature."

"Right, sorry, I just thought ..."

"It's alright, Douggy Boy. What I wanted to say was, err, what again?. Oh, yes, I don't want this feeling to be numbed by chemicals. I'm not in shock like yesterday. It's more like, ... I don't know, ... a feeling of ... amazement, ... awe." Vicus stroke his well kempt beard. "It's like a circle has been completed, yet, ... there are now more questions than before. And I don't know if they will ever be answered."

"Yes. We might never know the full story. But at least we are in contact with your sister's family now and together we can put some of the puzzle pieces in place. And as soon as Daniel has Whatsapped me the number of Annika in Maastricht, we can call her too. I'm sure she'd be delighted to hear from you again. Why did you stop corresponding with her?"

"I don't really know. Got busy, life went on, memories faded, you know. When Daniel mentioned her name, for a moment I did not know who he was talking about."

"Yes, I know." Doug thought of Rhoda. Memories of her have faded, but will never be gone. She will forever be in his heart, even though his mind had stopped being with her constantly. He still missed her and he knew his boys did too. But they have moved on and have learned to live without her.

The next day Doug called Grieta, who was over the roof with excitement. He told her in short all that had happened during the past couple of days. Annika was right there and he spoke to her as well. Then he gave his phone to Vicus and yet another emotional reunion by phone took place. The circle was now closed. If only Janneke was still with them to join in and share the joy.

****

A month passed with the three parties not only talking on the phone, but Skyping frequently. It was great to have contact with people they did not know existed, only a few weeks ago. Still, something nagged at Vicus's mind. He wanted more. More than just a voice on the phone or an image that hardly resembled any face he could remember. Annika was too far, but Daniel and his sister were within reach. Why could they not come and visit? He was pining to see them, to touch them.

That Saturday he mentioned it to Doug and Doug promised to invite his cousins. Daniel apologized and said he was too busy with a new project for his company but if finished on schedule, he might make the trip over the next school holidays. His sister is in a way self-employed and she might be able to go down at short notice. He promised to suggest it to her.

****

On Sunday Sharon and her daughter had lunch with Daniel and his family. During the meal, Daniel mentioned that Doug invited them to visit. They discussed it lightly, then, concentrated on the feast prepared by Margot, Daniel's wife. As soon as they retired to the patio where Margot served desert, the discussion continued more seriously.

"Come on, Sis, the old guy wants to see us and I am stuck in this project. You know I won't be able to leave for the next two months, six weeks at the least."

"What about Jacqui? I can't take her out of school and I can't leave her here on her own. Why don't we all go together just for a weekend?" Daniel rubbed his chin. "Now there's a thought. A weekend would be better than nothing. Then later we can go for longer. Maybe stay for the school holiday."

"Sharon, I have an idea," Margot said. "Why don't we all go for the weekend, bring Jacqui back with us and you stay longer? Jacqui can stay with us. I drive our children to school, I can take her too. No problem." Daniel and Sharon looked at each other.

"Are you sure, Margot, you don't mind?"

"Of course not. It will be a pleasure to have her. We don't see her often enough."

"She has ballet twice a week. You wouldn't mind taking her for that too?"

"As I've said, it will be a pleasure. Is it settled then? Shall I book us a flight?"

"Yes, I suppose," said Sharon looking questioningly at Daniel.

"Sure. Great. Let's go see the old guy before it's too late. Considering what happened to Grandma we better do it as soon as possible."

Chapter 8

The Visit

It was a happy six that stepped down from the plane at Durban's international airport that Friday afternoon. Happy, but also apprehensive.

Daniel parked the rented seven seater SUV in the driveway of the house in Amanzimtoti. Before he could knock, the front door opened and Doug welcomed them in. By now, Doug knew how Jacqui was the one who had traced the origin of the picture back to Holland and how they learned about the identity of the man whose face was circled in red.

"So this is the clever detective. A pleasure to make your acquaintance, Young Lady," Doug said with a smile as he shook her hand. He took Sharon's hand, looking intently into her eyes.

"Hello Cousin," he said, forgetting to let go of her hand. "Isn't God good to bring us all together?"

"Yes, God is good, all the time." For goodness sake, Sharon, when did you start talking in clichés, she thought to herself. Even though what she said was true, God is good, she could have said it in a more original way.

They all sat down in the spacious living room and Doug offered refreshments. He went to the kitchen and placed his order, then called out to his sons in the backyard to come in and meet the cousins. His sons were about the same age as Daniels children and the four left for the backyard, hitting it off as if they had known each other since always. Jacqui, a little more grown up, stayed with the parents and answered their questions of how she managed to trace the picture's origin and what followed.

A uniformed Zulu woman with a friendly face entered and served them with juice, soft drinks, pastries and biscuits.

"Mirjam, these are my cousins I told you about. Finally we get to meet them. You guys, meet my trusted house keeper, Mirjam".

They all said hello to Mirjam and how glad they were to meet her. After the greetings, Mirjam retired to the kitchen and the discussion on the topic of Vicus and Janneke resumed. Each one had a theory and an opinion of what happened to get the two separated and what happened afterward. They asked each other some getting-to-know-you questions, and, since it was late afternoon, it was decided that they would all meet on Saturday morning when Doug would take them through to his grandad's retirement village.

They left for their hotel, but Daniel chose the beach road and parked under a shade tree at a picnic spot close to the beach just outside the town of Amanzimtoti, the Zulu word for "sweet water". The youngsters, including Jacqui, ran for the beach while the grown-ups walked to the closest beach cafe, soaking in the humid heat of the Natal coastal climate.

"Boy oh boy, this heat is something," Daniel said.

"I kind of like it. There is something special in the air for me. I love Natal, the climate, the lushness of the vegetation, just everything." Margot agreed with her sister-in-law:

"Me too. I don't know if I'll survive January in this place, they say it is at its worse then, but now, in March it is just lovely to be here." In silence they listen to the breaking of the waves on the sand, the soft voices of the people around them, everything seems to be peaceful this time of the day. The youngsters were told to watch the sun. As soon as it dipped behind the horizon, they were to return to join their parents. They all agreed to have supper right there and then return to the hotel.

Early the next morning they gathered the children together and went down to the dining room of the hotel. They ordered a hearty breakfast of fresh juice, eggs, bacon, sausage, fried inions, fried tomato, fried mushrooms, hash browns, toast and coffee. Back in their rooms they quickly brushed their teeth, gathered their sunglasses, then got in the SUV and drove over to Amanzimtoti. Doug and his sons were waiting when they arrived. He led the way to Berea where his grandad stayed.

Vicus was overwhelmed at the sight of his sister's grandson, granddaughter and their children. Doug helped him out of his wheelchair and made him comfortable on the couch. Sharon and Daniel sat down on both sides of him to be as close as possible. Jacqui sat down on the carpet by his feet. At his request, she repeated the story of how she traced the picture back to Holland and eventually made contact with Annika. Tears dropped down his beard when Sharon showed him the picture that was in Janneke's hand, the last thing she saw before leaving this life. Sharon put her arm around his shoulder and hugged him tightly, sobbing with her head on his chest. Doug watched Sharon and his heart turned around in his chest. Such compassion from someone who just met his granddad. He found it quite touching.

Vicus told all he could remember and answered many questions. In return, Daniel and Sharon answered as many of his questions as they could. After three hours of reminiscing, Doug realised the old guy was exhausted, both physically, but emotionally more so. It was mutually agreed that they would leave Doug with him while he took a nap. They rest of the party including Doug's sons, was to go to the beach to cool down in the ocean.

As it was the worst time of the day to be outside in the sun, they decided to take a walk through the botanical gardens first. The foliage of many tall trees and plants form a canopy high above the many sidewalks, provided shade against the burning sun. Only a soft greenish light penetrated the leafy covering, creating the feeling of walking in a forest. The children particularly enjoyed discovering interesting plants they never imagined existed.

As the day advanced and the sun passed its summit, it was time to hit the beach. They all would just have a quick dip in the water and get back under the shade somewhere. Daniel parked in a safe spot on the Addington Beach front. In the public change rooms they quickly changed into their swimwear, applied sunscreen excessively, and made for the water. The tide was in and the tidal pool was in deep water, enough to have a good splash.

An hour was enough to create healthy hunger pangs and after drying in the sun for ten minutes, they dressed and headed towards the closest coffee shop for a light lunch. Salad was the popular item on the menu and chicken, tuna and bacon salad was offered, ordered and served: five chicken; two tuna and one bacon-salad, followed by fruit salad with vanilla ice cream. And now it was time to go back to Vicus who must have had a good rest by now.

Vicus was once more glad to see them. They talked, but avoided the painful issues of the past. After coffee and biscuits, they made sure Vicus was calm and strong enough to stay alone. Doug alerted the staff of the frail care unit who was supposed to react instantly in case of emergency. Doug also made Vicus promise to call if he needed anything.

"Call me, call me, call meeeeee," Polly said. The bird was quiet all through the hottest hours of the day. It was as if he suddenly woke up, and made his voice heard, to the utter delight of the children. They left, Doug leading the way back to his house where they planned to put some wors and chops on the braai. While Sharon was inside in the kitchen making salads and Jacqui buttering some rolls, the two cousins took care of the braai. Doug asked many questions about Sharon, her daughter, her life in general. He also touched the subject of her being single. Daniel loved his sister and did not mind talking about her. But at Doug's last question about her being single, he cocked his head and stared at him curiously. Why would he want to know about that? It is very sensitive and very private issues.

At the table, Doug pulled out a chair for Sharon next to his own. He became aware that he was uncomfortable in her presence. Sitting next to him, he could avoid looking her in the face all night long. But he wanted her close to him. With all the emotional experiences of the day, he had no energy to analyse this strange reaction in his chest every time he came close to her.

Sharon found it strange that Doug placed her next to him at the table, but did not show the discomfort it caused her. Nine people at a table meant for six, left little space between the seats and Sharon was careful not to have physical contact with her neighbours, Doug on one side and his son, Timothy on the other side. Next to Timothy, his brother Samuel was squeezed in on the corner, next to Daniel, then Daniel's two children, Jason and Janie on both sides of Jacqui. Margot was placed at the head of the table across from her husband. Sharon tried not to analyse the placing of each, which she realised, was deliberately done by Doug.

It was much later that night that she asked herself, why he didn't place Daniel close to him, so the men could have their men's conversations and the women closer together. And why did he place Jacqui across from himself? Though she noticed how he watched her during the meal and listened when she spoke, he did not talk much to her. What puzzled her most was her own reaction. Why was it so unnerving to sit so close to him? Twice their hands touched during the meal and each time she shied away, but hoping for more, wishing the next touch could linger. It is all the stress and emotion of the past few days, she told herself. Emotional exhaustion can do strange things to a person's inner workings.

The next day, Sunday, they all had a hearty breakfast at the hotel, then drove to the retirement village again to see Vicus. They knew the way, so they did not have to wait for Doug to take them. They spent a few hours with him, then said good bye with the promise to visit again as soon as possible. Vicus was sad at their departure, but consoled at the thought that Sharon would stay till the end of the week.

Their visit to the Verbeeks was concluded with a feast prepared by Mirjam, who was asked to work on Sunday. She was more than willing to do so for three reasons: to show off her cooking skills, double pay and a day off during the week, and she was curious, Doug told them as he showed them into the dining room. This time Doug's boys and Daniel's children were seated at the kitchen table, which left enough room for the five at the dining table. After a pleasant time together, Daniel, Margot their children and Jacqui said goodbye inviting Doug to visit them in Johannesburg and promising to come again during the coming school holidays.

At the airport Sharon waved good bye as they went through the departure gate. She watched until their plane disappeared, turned and went back to the car rental office. Daniel had returned the SUV and Sharon hired a small sedan which she now came to collect for the week. They had also booked out of their hotel. Sharon had to find new accommodation closer to Vicus.

She drove slowly, using the GPS to guide her. About two kilometres from Vicus's place, she found a guest house and booked a suite for the week.

Chapter 9

Falling

Sharon was having an early supper in the dining room of the guest house when her cell phone rang. It was Doug inviting her to have dinner with him and his sons. Why, oh, why did she decide to have an early supper? Here she was alone in a strange place with not one familiar face. Of course she had to decline, but oh, so reluctantly. On the other hand, it had been a long day. A day in which she had begun to feel very uncomfortable in Doug's presence. It was no longer her imagination. There was something about the man that made her want to run. Run from him? Run to him? Both, actually. Very confusing. She convinced herself in the morning, after a good night's rest, she would feel differently and everything would be normal again. But it was not.

The first thing she thought when she woke up very early was that it was Monday and she would not get to see Doug. He would be working. What a drab day it would be. Not even the idea of spending the whole day with Vicus and his parrot could stir up any amount of excitement in her inner parts. With heavy heart and feet, she dragged herself out of bed and into the bathroom. After a quick shower, she would have a light breakfast, just a light one. No appetite, see? And then she would go to Vicus to spend the day with him.

He phone interrupted her thoughts. It was Doug.

"Hi, sorry to bother you so early, but I was wondering. Would you like to go for an early dip in the ocean?"

"Aren't you working today?"

"I'm not expected at the office before nine. It is now six-o-five. If you'd like to go swimming with me, I'll wait. I'll give you ten minutes to get out of bed."

"Excuse me, I'm already showered and dressed and on my way to breakfast."

"They don't serve breakfast before seven. But since you're up, I'll give you one minute to join me."

"Where are you?"

"Right here in the foyer of your guesthouse. Grab your bikini and a towel and come. You won't regret it." Suddenly excitement was running amuck all through her insides. Gone was the drab, hello happy day! Two minutes later he helped her get into his car and they reached the beech with the sun scattering gold over the water.

At first the water was cool, but refreshing. As her body got used to it, the water felt warmer and they swam and splashed for almost forty minutes until hunger drove them out of the waves. Dried and dressed Doug drove them to a coffee shop up north in Marine Drive. The city was wakening and there were car guards on duty. Sitting across the table from him, pulled back the awkwardness between them.

Sharon studied the menu, as did Doug. They ordered, Doug said grace, they ate carefully not to make eye contact and the little conversation there was, came strained and out of rhythm. When he dropped her off at the guesthouse, Sharon got the impression he wanted to say something. He shook her hand, tried to grab it again after he'd let go, then turned away and left. She wanted him to say something and was disappointed when he did not.

'Pull yourself together, woman,' she told herself. What is wrong with you? He is only your cousin, he is not the president. Why the discomfort in his presence? Why did she get the impression he was scared of her? Sort of? As if she was the president. Well, look at the time, she kept on talking to herself. Vicus is waiting. She'd better hurry up. No time to ponder on Doug's strange attitude. Or her reaction, for that matter. She quickly took a shower, washed the ocean out of her hair, dressed in fresh clothes and drove to Vicus.

He was sitting on his patio talking to Polly when she arrived. It was already mid-morning and time for tea. He offered to make tea, but she insisted on making the tea and serving it on the patio. Before she could switch the kettle on, a grey haired lady walked into the kitchen with a tray packed with pastries and biscuits.

"Hello, I'm Celeste, the neighbour. You must be Sharon. So nice meeting you. Vicus told me yesterday you were coming to visit again today, so I brought something to eat. I'll just put it down here and slip out again."

"Hello Celeste, good to meet you too. And thanks for the goodies. But why are you in such a hurry? You should join us."

"Oh, no, thank you, but I don't want to impose. You and Vicus have so much to talk about."

"I assure you you're not. Please stay and at least have a cup of tea with us. It would be nice to get to know you better. Besides, I'll be here till the end of the week. So, Vicus and I have plenty of time to talk."

"Well, thank you, if you insist."

"I do. If you don't mind taking the eats out to the patio, I'll be there with the tea in a minute." Celeste left the kitchen with the tray and joined Vicus on the patio. When Sharon joined them outside, she heard them talking about Celeste's husband who was in bed with flu. She didn't want him to be alone too long, but he was sleeping, so she felt free to spend a little time away from home. Besides, home was a stone throw away. If her husband woke up, he could just yell, if he had a voice to do so, and she'd come running to his aid. Sharon poured tea and sat down. They chatted until the tea cups have cooled, Celeste excused herself and left. The rest of the morning, Vicus talked about the old days in Europe and England, telling many tales of the war and after, his life, his late wife - the first one - his sons and the move by ship to South Africa.

Vicus also told her about his sons, Gerhard, Jonathan and Stephen. Gerhard lived in Canada, Jonathan in New Zeeland and Stephen died of cancer many years before, his wife remarried and lived in the Middle-East. He saw their children once every three years when they come to visit. There are two great-grandchildren whom he had seen twice. Doug had three cousins, all living overseas. He was the only one who was there to take care of Vicus.

After they had lunch Sharon helped him to his room for his nap. She promised to come again the next day. She went straight home to make some phone calls. First of all she called her daughter, spoke to her sister-in-law also and learned that all was well. She made a few business calls too and then powered up her laptop to catch up with work. Being self-employed did not mean she could take as much time off as she liked and not keep the finger on the pulse. Hard work and diligence was what got her where she was and to neglect responsibilities might cost her too much of what she had worked for. Before she knew it, it was time for dinner.

She brushed her hair, put a fresh dress on and headed for the dining room. What an exciting prospect it was, eating alone, she thought, ironically. What if Doug showed up and invited her to dinner. Wouldn't that be nice? But Doug did not show up. Back in her room she switched on the TV and flipped from channel to channel until she found something she liked. Just then her phone rang. It was Doug explaining how much he'd like to see her, but he was stuck at work and wouldn't be able to leave till very late.

"How about an early swim again tomorrow morning?" he asked. "Can we make it a date?"

"Yes. I mean, no, I ... "

"Please, ... "

"Well I err, I ... pff, Okay, yes we can go for an early swim," she said, avoiding the word 'date' at all cost while touching her hot cheeks. For goodness sake, why am I reacting like a teenager she asked herself when she felt the fluttering feeling in her stomach.

She could hardly contain her excitement while getting ready to meet Doug. It was like her first date when she was sixteen. Judging her image in the mirror as if she were going to a formal ball, she took care of every little bit of detail about her appearance. It had to be perfect. Careful, she warned herself, don't overdo it. You're going for a swim, not to the opera house. When the missed call came to tell her Doug was waiting in the foyer, she was finally satisfied. She looked pretty, but casual.

Following the routine of the previous day, they splashed in the water until they were both starving. Lying on their beach towels to dry, Sharon was shocked to see the time. It was nine fifty seven. She jumped up and grabbed her towel yelling:

"Doug, look at the time. You're late for work."

"No, I'm not. I worked till late last night, so I can take the day off. In fact, I took the whole week off. So, relax. We'll have brunch at the beach café and then, well, you choose."

"What about Vicus? I promised to go and see him today."

"I know. I told him we'll see him later." Doug was on his feet too and took her arm to help her across the warm, loose sand.

Dried and dressed, they sat down in a booth by the window with a view of the sea. The discomfort of the previous day was gone. They were carefully becoming more open towards each other. Conversation came easy and they discovered they had a lot in common. At some point, Doug put down his fork, looked her in the eyes and said:

"Sharon, I'm so glad you are here." He took her free hand in his, rubbed her fingers gently with his thumb and smiled. "I am very glad you are here"

"Doug, I, ... I had to come. Vicus, ... he's old. You never know, ... "

"No, I mean I am glad you're here. For my sake. I'm falling for you. Haven't you noticed?" She took a sip of coffee, not because she wanted coffee. It was to partially conceal her face. And to give herself time to compose herself.

"You're overworked. Your imagination is playing games with you. We're cousins. You cannot ... we can't."

"My imagination can play games with me, but not with you. Don't tell me you don't feel the same."

"I think it's time to go." She took the serviette, blotted some imaginary something from her mouth and grabbed hold of her bag. Doug pressed his lips together, but was not about to give up so easily. Once outside he strolled back to the beach, guiding her gently with a hand in the hollow of her back.

"Let's just walk a little more on the sand. Give me your shoes. I'll carry them. Soon it will be too hot to walk anywhere outside. It's almost noon." Sharon relaxed thinking Doug would not pursue what he started during the meal. They walked, talked and any awkwardness there might have been, quickly disappeared. She laughed at his quips about strange people at work, she told him a few things about her career while they watched some ships lying out on the water or moving slowly to eventually disappear over the horizon.

Later Doug drove to his grandfather's place, dropped her off and promised to collect her for supper with his boys.

Chapter 10

Inappropriate Romance

Was it only a few days ago that she could not help but feel uncomfortable in Doug's presence? The way he looked at her. The way it made her feel when he looked at her. She had not known excitement like that in a long time. His touching her hand, or her arm when helping her out of the car, or his hand on her back going up the steps made her skin react in a strange way; warm all over. What was the matter with her? He was her cousin, for Pete's sake. Still, she could not resist when he invited her for a swim and to have brunch with him again the next day at the beach café. Besides, she could not think up one single valid excuse why not to. As long as he did not bring up his feelings again. She might not be able to resist again.

Yesterday he declared his feelings for her. Are they both mad she thought while their feet were kicking up water and sand behind them on the warm beach, the water lapping at their ankles. He took her hand, they chatted about nothing important. They stopped to watch a ship coming in. He moved in behind her and put his arms round her, his chin on her head. She should have moved away then, but did not, could not. As the ship disappeared behind the harbour wall, he turned her around, pulled her closer and kissed her gently on the lips. Her arms automatically circled his waist and she kissed him back.

"Doug, what are we doing?" she asked when he let go of her.

"I'll look it up in the dictionary, but I'm fairly sure it's called kissing."

"Beast," she said, but could not help smiling. "We shouldn't. We're cousins."

"Twice removed."

"Still. It's not right."

"You're right," he said, serious now. "It's crazy, but it happened to both of us. We both feel the same attraction. Don't we?" She looked away, not wanting him to see her expression.

"Yes. Both of us, it seems. How can it be explained? It really is crazy. And it must stop right now. This foolishness will end here and now. Please take me to my hotel." He pressed his lips together in a thin line and did not look at her. She did not look at him, just followed his lead to his car.

"Let's eat first." He drove to a coffee shop close to North Beach. The looks he gave her during brunch was unnerving, to say the least. His eyes penetrated her very soul, reflecting her own feelings. Lord, what is happening? How can we have this be happening? We're second cousins. It's totally inappropriate.

He wanted to talk to her, she could tell but apparently changed his mind. He just looked at her with a pained face that hurt her more that words of rejection would have. They did not talk much. There was not much to talk about. She finished what she came to do, that was to meet her grandmother's brother, tell him what she had learned, hear from him his side of the heart breaking story. She went back to say goodbye to him and told Doug she would be leaving earlier than planned. The same day, in fact. He wanted to protest, but she silenced him.

"Doug, let's end it here and now. Before it gets even more complicated. Before it gets more, painful." He took her hand and kissed her fingers.

"It's already as bad as it can get."

"No. The better people get to know each other, the deeper their feelings grow. Right now we are still on the surface, with solid ground under our feet. We can still walk away. We can still forget and move on."

"Do you really believe that? Can you really forget and move on?" One look into his eyes and she knew she could not. Neither could he.

"We have to. We have no choice, Doug. What good could come of this? We're not teenagers anymore. We know what's right. We know how important it is to do the right thing, not the nicest thing."

"Don't remind me. I could easily pretend to be eighteen, grab you by the hair and drag you to my cave." She could not help but giggle at this.

"You have a way of putting things, haven't you?"

"Sure. Want to hear some more of my ways of doing things? Serious now. I know you're right. Actually I'm trying to convince myself as much as you. I know it is too early to talk about love, but you do things to me that I have forgotten can be done to me. Even my sons like you. Do you know what Sam said to me? He said: 'Dad, I can see you like her. Go for it.' Now if that is not a sign." A hot glow rose up from her neck spreading crimson over her face and up into her hairline. She had not blushed in many years, did not know she still could. The last time an eleven year old boy could make her blush, was in the fifth grade.

"All the more reason to end it now. Before the children get attached and hurt."

"But why does it feel so right? Can you explain that?"

"No, I can't. Maybe there will come a time when we will know. Until then I will go on with my life in Johannesburg, you will go on raising your boys in 'Toti and we'll call each other a few times a year to say happy Christmas or happy birthday. And one day you will call me with the news that you have met a non-relative woman whom you are getting married to." He stretched across the table, took her hand again and pressed her palm against his lips. His eyes reflected her hurting.

"That, I assure you, will not happen. Rhoda is dead four years now. Killed by a drunken driver. Sam was hardly seven, Tim only four. I haven't looked at another woman since. You came and stirred emotions I believed was buried with Rhoda. The moment I saw you walking towards me from the steps in the foyer of that guesthouse, I knew something was going to happen. Actually before that. I think something happened to my heart during the braai at my house that very first day I saw you. And all because of a face in a fifty year old photograph."

"Yea. All because of that picture. They got separated, and now we have to also, get separated."

Back at the guesthouse he went up to her room, but she would not let him in. She insisted on saying goodbye in the hallway. He offered to take her to the airport later in the afternoon, but she refused. He wanted to take her in his arms one more time, but she pushed him away. It was over. Make a clean break and do it now. With his fingers under her chin, he lifted her face, kissed her gently on the lips, turned round and walked away.

After closing the door between them, she leaned with her forehead against the doorpost. A groan escaped through her lips as she turned around, leaning with her back against the wall, hugging herself. She touched her lips where she could still feel his lingering kiss. He walked away, out of her life. She will never see him again. She took five steps to reach the window, just in time to see his car starting up and moving out into the traffic. Too late to call him back. But why would she? There can never be anything between them. Better to forget and move on. How, Lord, how can I ever forget him?

She called reception and told them she would be checking out in five minutes and please get the bill ready. There was not much to pack. She grabbed her clothes from the closet, threw them on the bed and started packing them hurriedly. She checked the bathroom to make sure everything was neat and tidy, and nothing was left behind. Finally she zipped her bag, grabbed her handbag and left the unit. It was still early. Her flight would not depart in another five hours. That left her enough time to say good bye to Vicus.

****

Doug drove away deep in thought. He was sure his feelings for this woman, was genuine. And he got the strong impression that she felt the same. Though she never directly admitted it, she never denied it. It was in her eyes, in her kisses, all over her face. But how? She was his second cousin. They were not supposed to be attracted toward each other. He aimed to drive to the beach, but decided against it. The memory of Sharon and their kiss on the beach would be too painful. Without consciously deciding, he drove back to his grandfather's home.

"Hi, Grandad. I hope I'm not wearing you out with my visits."

"Never, my son, never. All visits are welcome, always. But why are you back? Is she gone? It was so good to have met her."

"Yea, she will be leaving in the afternoon."

"I know. She came to say good bye. Left minutes before you arrived. Why are you not seeing her off?"

"She didn't want me to. We said goodbye at her guesthouse." Doug pulled his fingers through his hair and looked at his grandfather, then through the window.

"Something wrong? You had a disagreement?"

"Grandad, I err, I ... "

"Why do you look so ... No, Doug, don't tell me ... you and her? Does she ...?"

"How is it possible? We are second cousins. It was not supposed to happen. But I'm sure she feels the same." The old man stared at the window, rubbing his beard. He looked at his grandson, looked away guiltily. Slowly he rolled his wheelchair round, into the bedroom, next to the bed and stopped in front of his nightstand.

His movements were slow and tired. He bent over and pulled out the bottom drawer, took out a brown envelope and without a word, handed the envelope over to his grandson.

"I should have given you this a long time ago. I promised myself I would wait for the appropriate time before I told the truth, but it got more difficult as time passed. The time just never seemed right. And why would it be important anyway. It shouldn't have affected your life. It hadn't, until now."

Doug took the envelope questioningly, opened it and pulled out some very old documents. It was the birth certificate of Stephen Farlow and some adoption papers. The birthdate was his father's. The adopting parents' names were Vicus Verbeek, and Kate Verbeek, born Dippenaar. Vicus, who he thought was his grandfather, was biologically not his grandfather. Vicus explained to him that his uncle Gerhard was his only son. Jonathan was the son of his second wife, Trudy. His father, Stephen Farlow was adopted in England. Shockwaves rippled through his whole being. Not believing what he saw in front of him, he looked up at his grandfather, his face one big question mark.

"My dad's adopted? So you are not my father's biological dad? And you are not my granddad, biologically?"

"No. I'm sorry. Please forgive me for not telling you earlier. As time passed, I sort of hoped it would never be necessary. Later I simply forgot. Your father was a war orphan taken care of by a distant relative, then dumped in an orphanage when she moved from Brittan back to Belgium to be with her family after her own husband died in the war. Grandma always had a heart for children. We fostered many, but your dad was too old to get adopted, so we kept him. We loved him as our own."

"I don't know what to say."

"Don't say anything. Get in your car and go to the airport." A light goes on for Doug. Smiling widely enough to display all his teeth, he kissed the old man on the forehead and jogged out to the parking lot, the envelope with documents safely in his pocket. He reached the airport safely, but in record time.

Two hours before her flight was supposed to leave. The check-in was not open yet. Where would he find her? He jogged through the departure hall, scanning with his eyes every corner and every coffee shop. She was sitting with her back to him, reading a book. He walked over, sat down opposite her. She looked up, straight into his eyes, the surprise clearly decorating her face. Lord, how beautiful she is, thank You that I found her, he prayed. He took both her hands in his, kissing them first one then the other. She pulled away.

"Please, Doug, don't, we ... " He placed a finger on her lips, then pulled the envelope from his pocket and put it down in front of her.

"Read this," he said. She took the documents from the envelope and stared in unbelief at them.

"So? Who is Stephen Verbeek, born Farlow?"

"He was my father. Granddad Vicus adopted him in England. He was a war orphan whom they fostered and was too old to get adopted, so they kept him and adopted him themselves, Granddad Vicus and his first wife, Kate."

"Why didn't you show these documents to me earlier?"

"I did not have them. After you shoved me out of that guesthouse I went back to Granddad. Didn't tell him anything, but he guessed. My face must have told the story. That was when he gave me the papers and even asked forgiveness for not telling me earlier."

"Did he say anything about me? You said he guessed, about us? Do you think he will approve?"

"No. He didn't say anything about you. Just told me to get in my car and drive to the airport." Her eyes sparkled and she smiled that heart-melting smile Doug adored so much.

"Well, what's next for us?"

"I'll beg you to cancel that flight and stay the whole week like you intended to do in the first place. I want to get to know you better. I'm sure you want to get to know about all my ticks and warts."

"Yes, and I suppose I'll have to tell you how Ben Hardy dumped his wife and baby girl to run to San Francisco after a cute blond American girl with blue eyes and dimples and never made contact again until the news came of his death by the hand of one of the girl's jealous lovers."

"That says it all. You can fill in the detail anytime you want."

"I doubt it. That's the whole story in a nutshell and the detail is of little importance. My daughter! She needs me ... "

"Your daughter is in good care and she expects you back on Sunday. Don't upset her now. She's having a good time."

"Well, let's go then. I have a flight to cancel. On one condition. Before we decide anything serious about the future you'll come and visit us in Johannesburg."

"And get permission?"

"Don't run ahead ... "

"Permission to date you."

"Yea, okay. To date me," she smiled. Arm in arm they left the airport to find new accommodation for her for four more days in Durban, close enough to the grandfather's, close enough to Amanzimtoti from where Doug, and his sons could take a short drive to pick her up for some get-to-know-my-ticks-and-warts-time.